MR. MURPHY'S MARVELOUS INVENTION

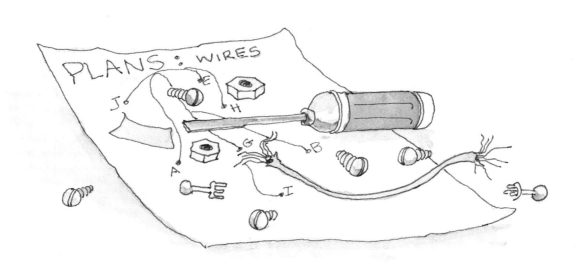

MR. MURPHY'S MARVELOUS INVENTION

STORY AND PICTURES BY EILEEN CHRISTELOW

CLARION BOOKS/TICKNOR & FIELDS: A HOUGHTON MIFFLIN COMPANY/NEW YORK

For Heather and Ahren

Clarion Books
Ticknor & Fields, a Houghton Mifflin Company
Copyright © 1983 by Eileen Christelow

Printed in the United States of America

Library of Congress Cataloging in Publication Data
Christelow, Eileen.
Mr. Murphy's marvelous invention.
Summary: Cornelius Murphy, a pig inventor,
makes a unique housekeeping machine for his
wife's birthday, but the entire family is
shocked when they discover what the machine
actually does.
[1. Pigs—Fiction.   2. Inventions—Fiction]   I. Title.
PZ7.C4523Mr.   1983   [E]   82-9594
ISBN 0-89919-141-X

Y 10 9 8 7 6 5 4 3 2 1

Mr. Murphy was an inventor of useful and not-so-useful gadgets.

The largest and most complicated gadget he invented was a birthday surprise for his wife, Mrs. Murphy. It took six months to build. He used three hundred screws, sixty yards of electrical wire, twenty-three switches, and a bottle of glue—among other things.

He allowed his children, Clotilde and Murdock, to help him with the finishing touches. Then he and Murdock wrapped the gadget with birthday paper while Clotilde printed a tag for it. The tag said: "A Very, Very, Very Happy Birthday to Ma. Love and Kisses from Pa, Murdock, and Clotilde."

The next morning, when Mrs. Murphy was cooking the breakfast oatmeal, Mr. Murphy crept up behind her and surprised her with a birthday kiss.

Murdock and Clotilde followed, pushing the birthday surprise.

"Happy Birthday, Ma!" they shouted.

Mrs. Murphy unwrapped the present.

"Oh!" she gasped. "It's very interesting. It's lovely. But ... what is it?"

"It's Pa's new invention!" said Clotilde.

"We made it ... Pa and us ... by ourselves," said Murdock proudly.

"But, what does it do?" asked Mrs. Murphy.

"I haven't tried it yet," said Mr. Murphy. "But it should do almost any tiresome household chore."

Mrs. Murphy looked skeptical.

Mr. Murphy attached the various attachments and plugged in the machine. He flipped a switch to ON.

The machine shook violently. Then it settled down to a quiet hum. Everyone watched expectantly, but the machine only hummed and whirred.

"It takes a long time to warm up," explained Mr. Murphy.

Murdock and Clotilde had to go to school and Mr. and Mrs. Murphy had to go to work before the machine finished warming up.

"Are you sure we should leave it on?" asked Mrs. Murphy as they left the house.

"Don't worry!" said Mr. Murphy.

When they returned home, they found the table set for supper. Pots were boiling on the stove and the oven was hot. The machine was still humming where they had left it.

"Someone cooked dinner!" said Mrs. Murphy.

"It works! Pa's invention works!" said Murdock and Clotilde.

"Of course it works!" said Mr. Murphy.

The Murphys sat down for dinner. Mr. Murphy served the soup.
"Looks weird," said Murdock. "Smells like soap," said Clotilde.
"I'm sure it will be delicious!" Mrs. Murphy smiled as she dipped a
spoon into her soup. "What a wonderful birthday surprise!"

"Ma!" shrieked Clotilde. "Look at your spoon!" Everyone looked at Mrs. Murphy's spoon. One of Clotilde's flowered tops was hanging from it.

"What's this?" asked Mrs. Murphy.

"Oh no!" groaned Mr. Murphy.

"It's laundry soup," giggled Murdock.

"I'm hungry!" wailed Clotilde. "What are we going to eat?"

They looked in the other cook pots, and they looked in the oven. But they only found more laundry, frying, boiling, and baking.

They finally found their dinner,
hanging on the washline.

Mr. Murphy stayed up late that night, trying to fix the birthday surprise.

Mrs. Murphy stayed up late, hoping he wouldn't be able to fix it.

Clotilde and Murdock stayed up late, whispering. They decided that Ma didn't really like the birthday surprise.

"And I don't like it either." whispered Clotilde just before she fell asleep.

The next morning Mr. Murphy woke everyone up. "It works!" he shouted. "I fixed it! The machine works!"

He showed them a pair of Murdock's pants. It had a patch sewed neatly on one knee.

"The machine sewed on the patch," Mr. Murphy said. "And it's doing the rest of the mending now."

The Murphys raced downstairs to watch. The machine had already completed quite a bit of work. The hole in Clotilde's dress was mended. Mr. Murphy's jacket was patched. Mrs. Murphy's sweater and Murdock's mittens were darned.

And they were all sewn together and carefully stitched to Mr. Murphy's easy chair. The easy chair was sewn to the curtains. The curtains were sewn to the sofa and the machine was still sewing.

"Turn it off!" screamed Mrs. Murphy.

"I'm trying to!" shouted Mr. Murphy.

"It doesn't work," muttered Mrs. Murphy. "It just doesn't work."

"But it will work!" said Mr. Murphy. "Every invention has a few wrinkles that need to be ironed out."

"And some inventions don't work at all," Murdock whispered to Clotilde.

Mr. Murphy continued to iron out the wrinkles for several more weeks.

He rewired the machine.

He put in some new parts.

He oiled it.

He even kicked it a few times.

But the machine continued to malfunction. It didn't make the beds very well.

It didn't wash the car very well.

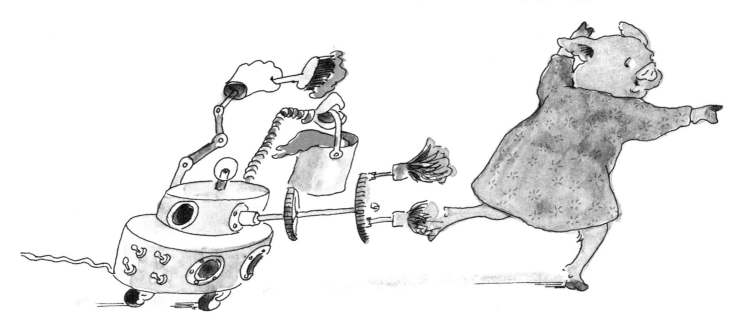

It didn't treat Mrs. Murphy very well.

Mrs. Murphy finally lost her patience. "Now you listen to me, Cornelius Murphy!" she said. "I've had enough of this contraption. It may be good for something, but it's not good for me!"

"That machine isn't good for Pa either," said Murdock. "He's awfully grouchy."

"But he won't give up," sighed Mrs. Murphy. "He just won't admit that this is one invention that doesn't work."

"I wish the birthday surprise would disappear. I wish it would blow up!" said Clotilde. "Or I wish someone would steal it!"

"That's unlikely," said Mrs. Murphy. "Who would want it?"

"Someone might," said Murdock thoughtfully.

Clotilde and Murdock spent the afternoon in their room. They said they didn't want to be disturbed.

Just before dinner time, a tall, unsteady figure with a big nose, glasses, a mustache and a floppy hat visited Mr. Murphy in his workshop.

"Are you the inventor of that incredible machine?" the visitor asked.

"I suppose I am," said Mr. Murphy, peering suspiciously. "Who are you?"

"Professor Mortimer," squeaked the figure. "I'd like to buy your machine. I'll show it all over the world. You'll be famous!"

"Oh?" said Mr. Murphy, squinting at the strange-looking fellow.

"I can give you two dollars and seventeen cents for it."

Professor Mortimer tried to reach his pocket, but his arms were too short.

He started to sway precariously.
"Stop that!" said a voice. "Help!" said another voice.

The Professor fell in a heap at Mr. Murphy's feet. Mr. Murphy stared in amazement. Clotilde and Murdock looked up at him from under the large overcoat.

Mr. Murphy chuckled. Then he laughed and laughed until he could barely breathe. Finally, still gasping, he went back to work.

Clotilde and Murdock hurried back to the house.

r. Murphy worked so late that night that he forgot to come in for dinner.

"Oh dear, oh dear, oh dear! When will he stop?" sighed Mrs. Murphy.

"Oh dear, oh dear, oh dear!" sighed Murdock and Clotilde. "Do you think we'll be punished?"

Just before it was time to go to bed, Mr. Murphy rushed into the house. He was holding a bouquet of violets and he was trying to hide a strange-looking contraption behind his back. He was very excited.

"Happy Birthday, my dear!" he shouted. "I just invented something wonderful for you, and this time it really works. Look!"

Mr. Murphy put the violets in a wind-up vase that revolved and played music at the same time.

"It's lovely," said Mrs. Murphy. "It really is! But … what happened to the other birthday surprise?"

"I sold it to Professor Mortimer," said Mr. Murphy. He winked at Clotilde and Murdock. "He's going to make me famous."

DATE DUE